COOPERS BRIDGE

Coopers Bridge

Written by Nicolaas A Gad

Self-published by

Nicolaas A Gad

albertgad67@gmail.com

ISBN: 978-1-7637114-6-4

First Edition: 2026

Cover design by Nicolaas A Gad

Printed in Australia

TABLE OF CONTENTS

ONE

“If I had a dollar for every time someone told me that, I’d be rich.”

“Yeah well I really think you should do it.”

“I might.”

They walked further along the path that wound down a steep hill overlooking a large valley. A large metal bridge, which connected this hill to the next, spanned the valley, and allowed trains to cross directly.

In the distance on the far hill, small figures moved towards the bridge. They walked along the train line, then made their way down to the underside, where a small walkway with railing allowed them to safely start crossing the valley.

“I wonder what they’re up to,” Steve said, “looks like they could be doing graffiti.”

“They have hoods, wouldn’t surprise me,” Gibson replied.

They both stopped to watch, observing the hooded men walk past the old graffiti on the side of the bridge, then stop, and face each other to talk.

The body language of the men seemed calm, and Steve and Gibson didn’t feel in any danger. They curiously watched the scene unfold, and their stillness let them remain unseen.

“I wonder what that ute is doing down there,” Gibson said, pointing at a ute in the middle of the valley, directly underneath the bridge.

“Could be someone going for a walk, I do wonder,” Steve replied.

The air was silent, and the view of the valley tranquil. The sun was low enough in the sky to add shadows with angles that gave depth to the scene. Quietly watching was a meditative pastime, as if life was a movie to be experienced.

“Woah what the fuck man!” Gibson shouted.

Steve looked, and could see a small figure in free fall making their way from the top of the bridge down toward the ute underneath. It soon hit the ground, bringing a small cloud of dust into the air.

There was only one man atop the bridge still, who began running back toward the side he came. And underneath, a man got out of the ute, lifted the limp body that had fallen, and placed him in the tray of the vehicle. He then moved back, entered the driver’s side of the ute, and drove off down the dirt road until he was out of view.

Remaining still, Steve and Gibson were unsure of what to do. Slightly shaking, yet still silently observing, they remained for some seconds before they turned and began making their way back to their own vehicle.

They got in and began to drive, and only when they reached far enough away to feel comfortable doing so, Gibson broke the silence.

“Should I call the police?”

“Fuck yeah you should call the police, man.”

He began to dial his phone, and quickly it was answered by an operator.

Gibson explained exactly everything that had occurred. Observing the valley, the hooded men, the ute, the fall, and the drive away.

And with only so much to go off, the operator took all the details they could, and the call ended.

Some hours later, they arrived at Gibson's house. Steve decided to stay with him for the afternoon, considering what they had been through together. They walked up the concrete steps that led to the front door, and went inside.

Gibson's house was in the centre of a dense suburb of government housing. He didn't work, and spent his days either with Steve doing anything to pass the time, or at home watching TV and achieving nothing.

Despite his poverty and lack of ambition, his house was tidy, his fridge had food, and he kept himself groomed. He was the type who waited for opportunities, but didn't create them, always assuming this was how life was played.

They sat in the lounge room with the TV off, and as the sun was setting and the light outside was fading, they rolled up a cigarette each, and talked.

"I don't think they saw us, at least," Steve said.

"Yeah I don't think so, lucky as fuck."

"What do we do from here?"

"Yeah I don't know. Seeing something like that makes me feel different, you know. But I think life just goes on the same. I mean, what more can we do?"

They sat for some time, thinking about what this would mean for them, if anything at all, and as Steve had one large drag from his cigarette, making sure to take in extra this time, he exhaled and raised his hand.

"Seems like something we could write about." He looked at Gibson and waited for a response, gauging if it was something he would be interested in.

"The scene did feel sort of perfect to describe," Gibson said, "could start with something like: They walked further along the path that wound down a steep hill overlooking a large valley. A large metal bridge, which connected this hill to the next, spanned the valley, and allowed trains to cross directly…"

"Good start. Like I said back at the bridge, I really think you should pursue writing. And now you have something to write about."

"Now *we* have something to write about," Gibson said, including Steve in this project.

As they finished smoking, they rolled another, and played some ambient music to accompany their creativity. They sat for some time in the lounge, discussing ideas and writing out the scene exactly as they remembered, and after only a few pages, it was complete.

They had described with beautiful accuracy from walking down the hill up until leaving in the car, and when it was finished, they looked at the paper in front of them.

"Cool, cool…" Gibson said, twiddling his thumbs.

"What should we do with it?"

"Maybe post it, or like, make up the rest?"

“What would come next though?”

“Maybe I’ll just post it, like a mini story.”

“Doesn’t really have any conclusion though, or anything. It’s more like a description at the moment.”

“Hmmm...” Gibson sat with his hand on his chin, thinking. He then moved his hand down to roll another cigarette, lit the end, and took a big inhale as his eyes focussed blankly into mid air, seeing his thoughts.

“If we frame it as a real story, then maybe it doesn’t need a conclusion, or anything like that. People will find it interesting anyway,” Gibson said.

“Yeah that’s true... it could be getting us more involved in this than we want though. Like people around here will recognise the bridge and the valley, and the people on the bridge will know we were there.”

“Hmmmm...” Gibson again sat staring blankly, looking at his thoughts, as he took another large inhale of his cigarette. “Unless, it’s anonymous.”

“Yeah okay... yeah alright,” Steve said while nodding, thinking through the idea.

Gibson took out his laptop, and began to transcribe what they had written on the paper into the computer, and when it was finished, he opened his social media, created an anonymous account, and posted it.

They smoked more cigarettes, and talked more in depth about anything that came to mind, and before long, they were both asleep on the lounges they'd sat.

TWO

The morning sun began to light the room through the window, and with a snore that got caught in Gibson's throat, he awoke, with a cigarette still between his fingers.

He looked around, then over at Steve, to see him still sleeping in a seated position with his mouth open and head back.

"Hghhhhh," Gibson groaned as he got to his feet, a sound he didn't always make but was increasingly doing as his health declined and age increased.

"Ugh!" Steve was startled awake by Gibson's groan, and he also looked around.

The birds began to chirp outside the window, and as the morning crept in, Gibson visited the kitchen to brew coffee. He returned with steaming mugs and sat back in his chair, across from Steve who still hadn't moved.

"Cigarette?" Gibson said as he passed a coffee to Steve.

"Sure," Steve replied.

They both sipped their coffee, placed their cigarettes in their mouth, and lit the ends, inhaling with a crisp burn. The silence of morning, and cigarette and coffee, was a meditation.

“Should we check the post?” Steve asked.

“Sure,” Gibson replied.

He took the laptop from beside him where he’d left it, and unfolded the screen from the keyboard, then paused.

“Maybe it’s best we leave it,” Gibson said, stopping mid motion.

“Why so?”

“I’m sure we'll hear about it if we need to. I sort of want to leave it all where it is.”

“Just check it, it’d be nice to know.”

“I think I’ll leave it, really.” Gibson was hesitating as he wasn’t used to anything out of the ordinary plainness in his life.

“Why the change of mind?”

“It’s too much, Steve. Too involved. What we saw was enough, but doing all of this now, making it bigger for ourselves. I don’t want any of it.”

“You’re freaking out man, relax. It’s too late, anyway, the post has been made,” Steve said as he looked at his phone, “and it’s been shared, and copied, and interacted with.”

“What do you mean?”

“Look…” Steve said, as he showed his phone to Gibson.

Ninety three shares. Police involvement. Hundreds of comments. All in the space of one night.

“How is this even possible?” Gibson asked, with slight concern in his voice, “take it back, Steve. I want to take it back.”

“It’s done, man. But we’re still anonymous. We have nothing to worry about,” Steve affirmed in a calm manner, trying to comfort the situation somewhat.

Gibson was silent, staring in front of him, before pulling out another cigarette from his packet, and passing another over to Steve. They lit the ends once again, and Gibson inhaled even deeper this time.

He exhaled with a deep sigh and relaxation, sinking into his seat.

“I guess we'll just have to wait and see,” Gibson said.

By the time the sun was adding heat to the day, they had become restless of sitting so still, and decided it was time to make a move.

“Hgghh eh egh egh!” Gibson groaned loudly as he got up, as if it was the most difficult thing to do.

“Haha,” Steve laughed, “why do you groan like that when you get up? You’re not even that old.”

“Yeah… not sure,” Gibson had his hand on his chin, thinking, “it’s not even hard to get up, just a habit I guess.”

“So ridiculous.”

“I think I copied it from my Dad. I’m very impressionable.”

They left the house, and walked down to the car parked on the street.

“Where are we going?” Steve asked, as he got in the passenger side.

As Gibson got into the driver's seat the car swayed side to side slightly, and he slammed the door shut with more force than necessary.

“Barista-made coffee?”

Steve smiled slightly and nodded.

For about fifteen minutes, they drove through the government housing estate, passing a mix of littered yards and well looked after lawns, until they came to the commercial space of shops, cafes, and restaurants that was nearby.

They got out, and walked the street looking for a suitable place, and when they found one busy and bustling with an energy that invited them in, they ordered and sat down.

“You know Dustin owns this joint,” Gibson said.

“Ah yeah… I haven’t heard that name in a long time,” Steve replied.

“The cappuccino, and the latte, lactose-free milk,” the waitress said as she placed the coffees on the table.

“Why lactose free every time?” Gibson asked Steve.

“Normal milk messes up my guts, not worth it,” Steve replied with his hand on his belly.

As he spoke, he heard the word “bridge” somewhere in the cafe. He raised his finger to let Gibson know not to speak, and looked with a focus that indicated he was listening. His mind filtered through the noise into the conversation.

“Yeah I saw that online, wonder if it’s real…”
“Probably just something someone made up, I saw the police page comment about it though.”

"Yeah only saying they are investigating the claim made by the post."

A daunting feeling of realisation washed over Steve.

"The police must know the post was us," he said.

Gibson paused, and his stomach dropped, as he had the same realisation wash over him, and then he spoke. "Are we retarded?"

"Nah nah, just got caught up in the moment with it all," Steve said, as he sat back and took a sip of his coffee, pinky in the air, and one leg over the other.

Gibson's lips pressed together in agreement, he nodded, and relaxed again.

They sat without talking for some time, enjoying their coffee and the environment, and listening to the chatter that surrounded them. And when they finished with their first cup, they ordered a second, and moved themselves outside.

Here they smoked alongside their drinks, observing the people who passed on the street, and sat with a feeling of indifference towards their situation.

"What's our next move? Do you have anything you need to do, or are you hanging with me?"
"Nah I'm pretty free," Steve said.

“Sweet,” Gibson paused, “should we check the bridge out again?”

Steve laughed, “so dumb,” he said while shaking his head. “Should we go to the station?”

“And do what?”

“I don’t know, might put some of this unease at rest. Touch base on it all with them.”

Gibson took his cigarette up to his mouth, pressed his lips around the end, and inhaled deeply, as if it helped him think.

His lips pursed, eyes squinted, and he nodded, as if agreeing took a lot of reasoning.

“Let’s go then.”

At the station, they waited for longer than intended, and when their patience began to wear thin, an officer arrived at the door leading to behind the desk.

“Can I help you?”

“Yeah we’re just here for… about the bridge, you know…”

“Okay. Come in.”

The officer led them in through the door to a room used for interviewing. It was small, with some chairs around a table at the centre.

“And what do you know about the bridge?”

“We uh, were the ones that called yesterday and explained it all,” Steve said.

“And the ones that posted about it then?”

“Yeah, yeah,” Gibson interjected, “we did. Just want to clear everything up from our side.”

“No problems. So let me get this straight. You went to the bridge, saw what you explained, then went home and posted about it on the internet anonymously.”

“Yeah that’s right.”

“Okay. That clears everything up.” The officer got up, put his notepad away and walked to the door, gesturing for the two to leave.

“Wait but, shouldn’t we explain more.”

“Nah no need to. We have found the suspects, found the body, the case is pretty much closed. Unless we find out anything we weren’t aware of, we have this under wraps. Thanks for your help.”

“Huh…” Gibson stared in front of him, surprised at how quickly everything had proceeded.

Steve and Gibson left the station with a feeling of lightness and excitement for it to be over.

They got in the car, and began to drive back to Gibson’s with small smiles on their face.

“What the fuck hey, craziest twenty-four hours I’ve ever experienced,” Gibson said.

Steve laid back in his chair, elbows up with hands on the back of his head, and a smirk he couldn’t remove. “Yeah man, crazy time hey.”

“Should we get drunk?”

“Better, let’s get fucked up,” Steve said with a wink, “pull over at Caleb’s on the way.”

About half way towards reaching Gibson’s, on the edge of the government housing estate, they stopped in at a small house. It was plain and had a brown tiled roof, with long grass and a cracked concrete path leading to the door.

They both got out, and walked up to knock.

The handle clicked unlocked, the door opened, and they were invited inside.

THREE

Caleb was a man with crooked eyes, and appeared aged from years of drug use, but not in the way of most addicts. He was a tripper.

He smiled widely with an energy that exuded non-physical places. He had curious and inviting yet eerily odd and strange vibes. The type of person that had thoughts no one ever thought of, and nonsensical phrases that somehow held meaning.

“A nap sandwich is the newest. Sound familiar?” he asked with confidence that Steve and Gibson would understand.

“It, for some reason, does sound familiar.”

“When the thoughts overlap in such a way they sandwich onto themselves, some get tucked between where we can’t see them anymore, hence the nap.”

“Hmmm,” Gibson pondered on it with his hand on his chin, “yeah I can see that. Like a fold of thoughts.”

“That’s right,” Caleb nodded adamantly and smiled, bearing gapped teeth that projected from his mouth, “you’re lucky you caught me in time, I was just having some salvia… not enough to take me out yet though, I think…”

“We just wanted to get some acid if you have any?” Steve asked.

“Sure sure… acid yep…” Caleb began opening the drawers of his cupboard, looking through bottles of powders and liquid to find it.

“What we have here gentlemen,” he said with grandiosity as he pulled a bottle of clear liquid from a shelf and held it up in admiration, “is the cleanest, yet strangest, type I have come across so far.”

“What do you mean? Isn’t it all the same?” Gibson questioned.

“Yeah well, no. It depends where it comes from, strength, how it’s made… slight variations exist.”

“Right right. Okay well how much for like, the two of us for tonight?”

“Couple drops if you want to go deep. I know you guys… should be fine with a couple drops.”

And so they received it blotted onto paper, and wrapped in foil, to slide into their wallets, out of sight.

Before they could leave, Caleb stopped them at the door.

“What’s the reason for the event?”

“Well…” they looked at each other as if considering whether to tell him. “We’ve been through a lot the last twenty four hours, need a reset.”

“You didn’t kill anyone did you?” Caleb said with a cheeky smile.

There was silence, before Caleb slapped Gibson on the shoulder and laughed, “just kidding mate, relax. Unless you did?” Another pause and stare off, “just kidding haha,” he laughed again.

“We saw someone get killed.”

Caleb’s smile turned serious, his eyebrows lowered, and stare intensified.

“You’re not kidding.”

“Yeah man, just want to get it out of our heads. Then we wrote online about it, it blew up, caused all this stress.”

“Hey hey,” Caleb said in a supportive tone, noticing the crackling voice of Steve about to shed tears, “stay here, I’ll guide you through it all. I have experience you know, I can help you.”

They returned to the lounge where the many drawers were and sat.

“So this is to do with Coopers Bridge,” Caleb said. He was the first to refer to it by its real name.

“Yeah, Coopers Bridge… apparently the case is solved, we just got back from the station.”

“Quick to be solved so easily. I wonder how they did that,” Caleb questioned in a tone that implied suspicion.

“I thought the same,” Gibson said, “was a little bit stunned when they told me.”

“Well… let’s get into it then,” Caleb wasted no time.

He rubbed his hands together, and grabbed the bottle of acid from the table again.

“Mouths open,” he said. Gibson and Steve did as he said. Caleb held the small bottle between his index and thumb, pinky in the air, and carefully dropped two drops into each of their mouths.

Caleb added some ambient music, good vibes, and tidied the room. Before long, the pictures on the walls began to move, in a way that resembled the wind on cloth.

“I want you to recall exactly what happened, the scene as close to what you remember,” Caleb asked.

They thought for some time, trying to imagine the scene exactly.

There it was, Coopers Bridge stood strongly over the valley, the hills and picturesque sky vivid in their imagination.

The hooded men walked to the bridge, and disappeared underneath to the walkway.

The ute sat underneath, still and awaiting the fallen victim.

“I see it as it was, right there in front of me,” Gibson said, staring into space as if seeing his imagination there in the real world.

“Now what?” Steve said, staring in the same way.

“Aaannndd mouths open,” Caleb said, with his mouth open and up, showing them what to imitate.

They followed his direction, and Caleb again carefully and elegantly dropped two more drops into their mouths.

“Hold that image in your mind, and look for details you hadn’t noticed before.”

They did, and sat like this for minutes that quickly turned into close to an hour, and as the second dose began taking effect, the image became so clear it was as if reliving the moment exactly.

“I feel like I’m there, I can feel the wind, smell the air, hear the breeze,” Gibson said.

“Good, good, now look around.”

“I see, another car, to the left. Do you see it?”

“I see it too,” Steve said.

They squinted, trying to bring it into focus.

“Is that, Frankie’s car?” Gibson asked.

“Who’s car?” Caleb asked.

“Frankie’s. Steve is it?”

“It does look like it, would be strange if it was.”

They watched it sit quietly to the left, watching the bridge from below, close enough to also see the ute and the hooded men, but far enough to perhaps be out of sight.

They came back to reality after observing this new detail for some time, and slowly Caleb’s room came back into focus.

“So Frankie’s car, and you hadn’t noticed that there before?”

“No no, at least not consciously,” Steve said.

“It might not be Frankie’s car. It could be just one that looks like it,” Gibson made sure to not make assumptions.

“Well how about we call Frankie, huh?” Caleb said with a slow and bouncing cadence that added a playful yet answer driven force behind the words, as he looked side to side between the two of them, close to their faces.

Gibson stared back, on the back foot, then let the words out, “sure, yeah sure. Let’s call Frankie.”

Steve took out his phone and typed into his contacts Frankie’s name, and dialled.

It rang, and then answered.

“Frankie, my man. How are you?” Steve said in an overly confident tone.

“Don’t have to act cool, give me the damn phone,” Gibson said as he grabbed it off him.

“Frankie it’s Gibson, is now a good time?”

“Yeah mate, sure, what’s up?”

"You didn't happen to be at Coopers Bridge yesterday, were you?"

"Who's asking?"

"Well, just us, but we noticed a car like yours there, and just thought we'd ask."

"Where are you? I'll uh..." he paused, "I'll come around and we can talk."

Caleb gave a nod of approval, his smile widening as he enjoyed the growing mystery and network of events occurring before him.

They waited until a knock was heard on the door, and they let Frankie inside.

"Mouth open," Caleb said.

"What the fuck, what do you mean 'mouth open,'" Frankie said imitating Caleb's unusual tone when he repeated his words.

"It's acid," Gibson said.

"I don't want fucking acid, I came here to talk. Yeah I was at the bridge, what about it?"

"So you saw the guy fall?"

"Yeah I saw the guy fall. It was horrible. Really. I've been wanting to get it out of my head."

"Why were you there Frankie?" Steve asked.

"I uh... don't know really. Someone told me to go there, not sure what for, and I never found out."

"Who told you to do that?"

"I uh," Frankie's eyes looked at all three of them, with a worried and pressured look on his face, "I..."

"You're not under investigation or anything man. We were there too, just happened to be, we just want to find out what's going on here."

"I can't say guys, I really can't."

"Andddd mouth open," Caleb said, and before Frankie could disapprove this time, Caleb sprayed a substance into his face. Frankie breathed it in, coughed a little, and looked in shock that someone would drug him.

Before long his tense body relaxed, his eyes closed somewhat, and he seemed in an intoxicated way.

"Who told you to go there Frankie?"

"Tom, sweet Tom told me to."

"Sweet Tom?" Gibson and Steve looked at each other.

"Yeah sweet Tom. He called me and said to meet him there, that he was going to do some art, wanted me to watch."

"Sweet Tom?" Gibson questioned it again.

"Who is Tom?" Steve asked.

"Just a guy I know."

"Have you heard from Tom since?"

"I talked to him this morning, but not since then, haven't heard from him all day."

Frankie's words became more mumbled and softer, and his eyes slowly closed as his sentences dribbled into nothingness. He fell unconscious, and began to snore.

"What the fuck is going on here?" Gibson said to Steve.

Caleb's eyes were wide and his smile was bright. He so loved every bit of this real-life mystery.

"I think it's time to call it a night men. Hopefully you can find out who Tom is, and when you do, you can update me," Caleb said with his smile and enthusiasm.

“This isn’t a movie Caleb, but yeah sure, we’ll update you,” Gibson said to him.

They left Frankie there on the couch, and Caleb let them sleep in the spare rooms of the house. They had a bed each for the night.

And when the moon left and the sun returned in the morning, they awoke and met in the lounge once again.

Gibson pulled his cigarettes out from his pocket, and slid one out of the packet for Steve.

They boiled the kettle, poured a coffee, and made their way to the front porch to smoke.

“Frankie’s still out hey?” Gibson said.

“I suppose he is. I wonder how long for.”

“We can wake him up after this.”

“Sweet Tom hey. Weird thing to say…” Gibson said.

When their cigarettes were done; and coffee half way empty, they went back to the lounge where Frankie laid.

Gibson went over, grabbed him by the shoulders, and began shaking and yelling into his face.

“Who the fuck is sweet Tom! Who the fuck is sweet Tom?!”

“Woah woah what the fuck Gibson,” Steve said, pulling him off Frankie.

Gibson laughed hard, as if it was the funniest joke he had ever pulled. It was hard for Steve not to laugh.

Frankie moaned and mumbled a bit, arms flailing from the immediate shock of the shaking, before opening his eyes and coming to.

“Sweet Tom?” he said.

“Yeah yeah, you know, the art guy,” Gibson explained.

“Oh right… how do you know about Tom?”

“You told us after Caleb drugged you last night.”

Frankie sat still, stunned at the honesty in the room.

“Fair enough…” There was nothing else he could think to say. His arms retracted, and his body language signalled weakness and defeat.

“I’ll talk to him today, maybe you can meet.”

Frankie got up, stumbled up the hallway to the front door, and left.

The pair, Steve and Gibson, left shortly after, before Caleb had even awoken.

They now had new information to follow about the case. Tom, the artist, as far as the information they had, was likely one of the two masked men on the bridge.

“How do we find Tom?” Gibson asked, as they sat in the car outside of Caleb’s.

“He’s either dead, or a murderer, based on what we know,” Steve replied.

FOUR

Tom awoke, alarm sounding as he had a performance coming up soon, and so was getting up early to prepare.

He rolled from his bed, got to his feet, and walked to the window to open it. He lived in an apartment above the shopping centre in the main part of town. A modern white with plain walls and square finishes, it was a home of grand minimalism.

Preparation this morning involved the completion of a scale model version of Coopers Bridge, with the ute at the bottom, and two men directly above it, on the walkway underneath the bridge.

Once completed, Tom carefully measured out the distance the two men on the bridge were from the edge, and then measured his own average footstep distance.

He used these numbers to calculate how many steps to take on the bridge to be almost exactly above the ute. He knew he could eyeball it on the day, but his obsession kept him focussed on every detail. He enjoyed every bit of the process.

Once he had all the measurements finished, he called to advise the ute driver on how to park in the correct location, and everything was set.

Tom walked to his wardrobe, and inside, folded together under the hanging clothes, was a hooded jumper and a black cloth mask to cover his face.

He looked at them for a moment, mentally noting that putting these on was the final thing he needed to do before the performance, and then he closed the wardrobe.

He left his room and entered the next door down the hallway in his house.

“Morning Dylan,” he said as he flicked the light on.

“Ugh morning,” Dylan replied.

“Finally the day hey.”

“Yeah… it’s finally here…” Dylan stared in front of him.

“I’ve got your hoodie and mask, everything else is sorted out, and your family will be paid the money.”

“Perfect,” Dylan said, knowing all too well that this was the furthest thing from perfect.

They left the home at lunch time and headed for Coopers Bridge. They arrived on the far side to the town and parked some distance from the bridge, at a small electrical station that sat alongside the tracks. From there, they began to walk.

“Are you ready?” Tom asked Dylan as they walked.

“As ready as I’ll ever be,” Dylan replied, “and there is no other way?”

“No other way,” Tom said as he shook his head.

They approached the beginning of the bridge, where it lifted off from the ground receding underneath it, and followed the ground to the metal walkway.

Tom could see the ute beneath ahead, and began counting his steps.

When he reached the spot directly above the ute, he looked at Dylan.

“No value in savouring this moment,” Tom said, and then he grabbed Dylan by the armpits and shoved him backwards towards the railing.

Dylan’s mind began racing, as he felt the balance point of his body proceed further than he could recover, and he noticed the absence of a fall break as he started accelerating towards the ground.

The reality of his situation dawned upon him in more lucidity and clarity than ever before, and in his final moment he let go mentally, in full surrender, as he realised in its rawest that there are forces greater than our own, and there are things we cannot change.

As Tom made his way back to the car, he took out his phone for a moment and opened up his web browser.

There he could see a website in all black that showed several numbers, one labelled ‘total viewers’, one ‘total sales’.

‘Support the family of Dylan Stepple,’ it said there on the home page, ‘70c out of every dollar of profit goes towards Dylan’s family.’

FIVE

“So I got free entry, but usually it’s several thousand per person,” Frankie explained, “they do it once a month.”

“Some sort of sick art project god damn it,” said Gibson, slamming his hand on the table in front of him.

“Gibson mate chill out a bit,” Steve said.

Gibson smiled a bit, “sorry, go on Frankie.”

“So I went. I didn’t really expect it to be as advertised… I mean part of me worried, but to ever believe something like that could be real…”

“Do you have the website?” Steve asked.

“Yeah sure…” Frankie took his phone out and opened a link saved to his browser.

The website was still active, and advertised the total amount raised for Dylan’s family, alongside the next performance date and person ‘performing’.

“Three weeks, we can go to the next one, find out more about what’s going on here,” Steve said.

They all nodded in silent agreement, acknowledging the depth of their involvement now, and what they were going to witness in some time.

It was a few days that passed as everyone went on with their normal lives until Gibson had a revelation.

He had invited Frankie and Steve around to his house, where they sat in the lounge to talk.

"Who isssss…" he held the 's' for some time as he twirled a pen between his fingers while flicking through the pages of a notepad, as if it was some document of important information, "David Schwepps?"

Everyone in the room looked at each other, then back at Gibson for answers.

"David Schwepps was a performer. Note, 'was'."

"You mean for the fall performances?" Steve asked.

"That's right. Before Dylan Stepple."

"And what about him?" Frankie asked, "we know there have been at least forty performances so far. How'd you even find that out anyway?"

"We know that all information of previous performers gets deleted once a new performance has taken place. But I came across something called… 'The Way Back Machine'," Gibson waved his hand across in front of him as he said the name to present it with some aura.

"Ah yeah that's actually pretty smart," Steve said.

“What is it?” Frankie asked.

“It’s like a record of all of the internet history. It saves websites data and downloads their content so if one day it gets deleted there is still a copy,” Steve explained.

“So I looked back through at all of the past performances. David Schwepps. Danny Stallone. Deborah Stingfoot. Deep Swahili… you see what’s going on here?”

“All the initials are the same,” Frankie caught on.

“I wonder how many people there are with the initials D.S. in the city? And why those initials? So strange… random.”

“Not random, but good point Steve. Good questions. Great questions…” Gibson slightly exaggerating, “I wonder the same…” he introspectively stared with his hand on his chin, tapping his finger in thought.

“You think some more acid would help?” Steve asked.

“With that ‘mouth open’ guy?” Frankie said.

“Yeah Caleb. He might have some unique ways of interpreting all this,” Steve suggested.

“Shall we?” Gibson gestured at the door for them to leave.

They drove again from Gibson's to Caleb's, and as they parked on the street and got out, Gibson took out his packet of cigarettes and leaned up against the car.

"I'll meet you guys inside," he said as he sparked the lighter and lit the end of his cigarette.

Steve and Frankie went to the door and knocked, and got invited inside, and as the door closed behind them, Gibson stared at the house for some time, inhaling deeply for a moment of peace.

"What have you got yourself into Gib," he muttered to himself.

Something inside him knew his life now had more excitement and meaning than ever, and direction had seemingly come from nowhere. But he was scared on a deep level that he tried not to let show.

Gibson was used to safe and predictable, although he also knew this set of events was a calling for him to follow.

As he came to the end of his cigarette, he put it out on the car door, leaving a mark in the paint, and threw the butt into the gutter. He pushed his weight up off the car and walked up to Caleb's door, knocked, and entered.

Inside, Gibson could hear Frankie and Steve talking to each other while Caleb was at the door.

"Just tell him the full story man, you're the only one that knows this, and now me."

"But I feel like it's not relevant."

"It's all relevant Frankie… you know it is."

"What's relevant?" Gibson asked as he made his way to the lounge room.

They both looked at Gibson with silence, as if not knowing when to say it.

"Let it out…" Caleb said with a smile bearing his gapped teeth and a nodding head.

"It's how I met Tom," he paused and looked at the group. The space gave a sombre tone, and Frankie's eyebrows lifted in such a way that showed hurt in his heart.

"Dustin Stanford… we all know him, except maybe you Caleb."

"I've heard of him, yeah. He owns that cafe in town," Caleb said.

"We all used to know each other as kids. We'd ride our bikes in the afternoons after school. One time, we rode down to our usual spot by the train line where there was a small building next to the tracks."

Gibson's eyes closed; he looked down and his head shook as he acknowledged the memory. "I remember…"

"We climbed up the pipes aside the building, and onto the top. The roof was made of fibreglass, I remember we had to be careful not to place our hands on it or we'd get shards of it in our palms."

"That's right, I forgot that part," Steve said with a small smirk, appreciating the detail.

"Once up on the building, Dustin took his backpack off and brought it to his front, and unzipped it. He reached in and took out a small wedge-looking thing."

"What do you mean wedge?" Caleb asked. "Like a doorstop-type shape?"

"Yeah, like a door stop type of shape, made of metal," Frankie confirmed.

Caleb nodded, listening intensely as he visualised every detail of the story.

"We all looked at him wondering what it was for. 'It's to derail the train,' Dustin said to us. He climbed down the pipes of the building again, and we all watched from up there."

"I remember reading about the train…" Caleb said, "so you were there?"

"We all were, we watched it happen."

"I've tried to forget that day… What's this have to do with Tom, Frankie?" Gibson asked.

"Some months ago, I saw Dustin at his cafe. He came to sit with me out the back at one of the more quiet tables. We talked about what happened.

'Not many people have experienced something like that,' he said to me. 'But I know deep down, they sort of want to.'

'Sort of want to what?' I said.

'They sort of want to see something intense.'"

"So he started it?" Gibson asked.

"Yeah, with Tom."

Caleb again was smiling ear to ear, detached from being directly involved yet watching it unfold gave him a lot of pleasure.

Several days passed as Gibson, Steve, and Frankie spent some time apart, having a break from the ever deepening mystery of the Fall Performances.

SIX

Caleb spent his time doing his own things, dealing to those who wanted a taste of his vast collection of compounds, and spending time with those who wanted to interact with his interesting energy.

He rarely spent a day alone, and rarely spent a week without experimenting on his own mind. While napsandwich was one of the strange signature concepts he was able to articulate, he had many.

Silly Napstick Place he described as the destination he arrived to so often on dimethyltryptamine - a potent psychedelic. A land of a circus, a carnival of strange celebration. Inflatable freaks made of wax that rolled, and elegant jesters that controlled the time unfold.

"It's not every time that I smoke it, but so often I return there. I see the ribbon in front of the entry come loose as it opens. It really does feel like a carnival, with music of clowns and spiraled tents with checkered colours. And when all is done, and it starts to wear off, they wave me goodbye, and the ribbon gets hung again," he explained to Sonja as she considered whether it's really something she wanted to try.

"But it's not always like that is it? I've heard people meet God?"

"I've heard many different accounts. I'm sure there are many places in the realm. Some people find profound spiritual insights. I've had that too, deep and personal experiences, and then for some reason, also silly napstick place."

His fingers pointed and waved past the different draws of his cupboard, searching for the correct one to open.

"Mmmm.... Ah yes," he nodded as he found the right draw, and pulled it open.

He carefully reached in, where many small velvet covered boxes the size for rings sat in ordered rows. He took one from the draw, unclasped the small brass buckle on the front, and lifted the lid.

Inside sat a small cartridge of yellow liquid.

"You place this into this vaporiser here, turn it on and inhale. The easiest way to experience the substance."

"And how much is that?"

"I can give you this cartridge for two hundred dollars. And the vaporiser for forty."

Most of Caleb's interactions went this way. He explained his experience of what he was selling, along with some strange and abstract concept that had a name that sounded made up, and then offered them to purchase.

It's what made Caleb unique, and what kept bringing the same people back. And while he fit into his niche and embraced his character perfectly, there was a shallowness to the connections he made.

As soon as Sonja left, Caleb was left by himself again, inside where he mostly resided, with only the company of his own obscure mind.

He sat at his desk in the room next to his bedroom, and looked down at a pen and notebook he often wrote in. He turned the pages, past descriptions of strange things he had come up with or come across over the years, to find a new and untouched page.

"What does it feel like to have a real friend?" he wrote, "while I have people I know, I don't know the experience of laughing with someone about a common understanding. What is it to be understood or feel among a group. I've always felt I am a character for others to enjoy, rather than a person for them to connect with."

………

"Who does Caleb hang out with?" Gibson asked Steve as he welcomed him in.

"Not sure… probably has a group of trippy friends or something I'm sure. Never really thought about that."

"Yeah it just came to me. And it's like he never leaves his home…" he looked at the ground, tapping his finger on his chin, contemplating, “you ever think he wants to hang out?”

“We do hang out with him.”

“Yeah but beyond visiting him at his. Maybe he’d enjoy the adventure we’re on. I can tell from his smile he’s invested.”

“Next time let’s ask him,” Steve suggested, nodding in agreement as he thought about it more.

“What’s the approach for today?” Gibson asked on another note.

“Frankie’s busy, I spoke to him before.”

“Hmm…” Gibson tapped his fingers on the table in front of him, “cigarette?”

Steve nodded. They took one each from the packet on the table in front of them and lit the ends. For some time they sat in silence, enjoying the nicotine and letting their minds become open to ideas.

“So we have twenty days until the next performance,” Steve said.

“That’s right,” Gibson replied.

“And in that time, there doesn’t *feel* like there’s a lot more for us to uncover,” Steve said, emphasising the word feel.

“It sure doesn’t *feel* that way,” Gibson repeated the emphasis on the word feel.

“But the way we are saying *feel* implies that maybe there is something… we just have to figure out what.”

“That’s right,” Gibson affirmed again.

“Should we return to where it all began, maybe it will inspire us,” Steve suggested.

“That’s right,” Gibson repeated in the exact same way, staring blankly in front of him.

“Gibson?”

“That’s right,” he repeated once more with the exact tonality and cadence as before.

Gibson's blank face broke its steadiness with a smirk, and his eyes looked over at Steve.

“It’s not even that funny really,” Steve said, smiling but slightly annoyed.

“You enjoy it,” Gibson said, “let’s go.”

They made their way out of Gibson's house and down to the car. Again, once in the front seats, and seat belts buckled, Gibson took two cigarettes from the packet in his pocket and handed one to Steve.

They drove first to Caleb's house, where they knocked on the front door to see if he was home.

Caleb answered, pleased to see the two there.

"What can I help you guys with?"

Gibson smiled, took out his arm and patted Caleb on the shoulder.

"We want you to come along for a ride," he said as his arm found a place to rest on Caleb's shoulder and grabbed it to shake it in a friendly way.

"What for?" Caleb wanted to confirm to himself whether it was a job or spending time with friends.

"Just to hang out," Steve said, "if you want."

Caleb's smile widened in a different way this time, slightly smaller, flickering up and down at the corners in slight disbelief and acknowledgment.

They made their way back to the car and left again, travelling out of the government housing estate, and onto a main road that led toward Coopers Bridge.

When they arrived, they got out, and walked again along the path down the steep hill. They stopped for a moment only part way along from where they'd been last time, and looked at the bridge.

Gibson leaned in toward Caleb and pointed at the bridge in a way so Caleb could see what he was pointing at.

"They walked along here, from up there, with masks, and down here was the car," he explained to him while his finger moved to show where it all happened.

"Then they continued across, and about here we looked up and saw, it would've been Tom, push Dylan off, and…" he whistled as his finger moved downwards toward the ground, describing the falling, "he hit the ground here."

"Heavy…" Caleb said.

Caleb now had a clear image in his mind of what the crew had been describing earlier. He understood how everything played out, and how it would go at the end of the month.

After observing the bridge for some time, the three of them returned to the car, and drove back to Caleb's to drop him off.

"We'll touch base again closer to the next performance," Gibson said, "we can all go together if you like."

“Twenty days, I’ll make sure I remember,” Caleb said, as he walked up his front steps and entered his house.

“See you then,” Steve said to him.

And as Steve and Gibson got back in the car, Gibson spoke.

“I’m glad we brought him along… he’s a good guy.”

“Yeah, good guy,” Steve nodded in agreement.

SEVEN

Twenty days passed quickly, close to three weeks of normal routine. Gibson mostly stayed at his house, smoking cigarettes and every so often going out for drives with Steve. And when there were just two days left until the next performance, they began getting ready.

Gibson invited Frankie, Steve and Caleb over to his home to discuss the plan.

"I'm pretty sure we just turn up… I can't see why we'd even have to buy tickets," Frankie said.

"Maybe they check…" Steve suggested.

"I can't imagine it's something they'd be able to control…" Gibson said, "and they're not cheap."

Caleb sat in silence, listening tentatively and thinking.

"What if there are consequences for not paying?"

"I wouldn't worry so much Caleb, you'll be with one of us anyway," Gibson replied.

It seemed a straight forward plan. On the day, they would drive toward the bridge, find a good place to view it, and wait. And so when the day did come around, they all met at Gibson's.

It was a Wednesday, and Caleb was the last to arrive.

“All ready?” Gibson asked him.

“Yep,” Caleb replied.

They walked towards the car and all found a seat, Steve and Gibson in the front, and Caleb and Frankie in the back.

Gibson took out his packet of cigarettes.

“Cigarette?” He asked, and handed one to each of them.

With a cigarette in hand and a now smoky car they drove out of the estate towards Coopers Bridge.

It was still early, and cold outside, but from memory they had an idea of the time the last performance took place, and so anticipated it would be similar this time.

They parked the car some way from the bridge, on the same side they viewed the first time. They were within clear sight of it, at the top of the valley, but far enough to hopefully stay under the radar.

Once they parked, they sat back and waited.

“Coffee?” Gibson asked, as he pulled a kettle out from under his seat and plugged it into the cigarette lighter in his car to begin a boil.

“Yeah I’ll take one,” Caleb said.

“Me too,” Steve said.

“Yeah thanks Gibson,” Frankie also said.

“Milk? Sugar?” Gibson asked.

“Just black is fine,” Steve said.

The others asked for milk, no sugar.

Once the kettle came to a boil, he took milk out from under his seat as well and poured each a coffee.

“Cigarette?” Gibson asked.

Everyone agreed.

And so they sat with warm coffee in hand, and a cigarette to accompany them as they waited.

Before long, they noticed other cars begin to arrive. Across the valley they could see among the bushes cars creep in and find their place.

Down below also cars began to find their place, all pointed toward the bridge.

Then in the distance they could see two men walking along the tracks toward the far side of the bridge. They were hooded, and wearing balaclavas to hide their identity.

As the men approached the bridge, they walked underneath toward the footpath, and made their way toward the middle. And when they reached the middle, just as they could see one man lift the other and push him over the hand railing, they heard a knock on the window.

"Tickets… please," a man outside asked.

Everyone inside the car looked at each other.

"We uh, we don't have them," Gibson said as he ensured the doors were locked, then took a sip of his coffee.

The man looked at them in silence for some time, then pulled out a handheld radio.

"Hey Rod we have a car full here, can you ask Dustin what he wants to do."

"Copy."

"Fucking let's get out of here," Steve nudged Gibson.

Gibson turned the key and began starting the car.

kchchchchch

kchchchchch

“Fucking let’s go,” Steve said.

“Come on, cmon cmon,” Gibson repeated as he kept trying.

The man outside the car started punching at the back window to break it, and before Gibson could start the car, Caleb’s window was smashed open.

“This is your ticket,” the man said as he grabbed Caleb and pulled him out through the window of the car.

“Fuck,” Gibson said, as finally the car started. More men began turning up outside, and options were becoming limited.

“Let’s just go,” Frankie said, “there’s nothing we can do.”

“We can’t leave him,” Steve said.

Gibson didn’t say a word, and just began driving, wide eyed and mouth open in shock as to what he was having to do.

Caleb watched as they drove away, and when the car receded out of view, he looked at the men that surrounded him.

He had nothing to say, vulnerable and in shock as to what his situation now was.

They carried him towards the bridge, down underneath toward the footpath with railing. Caleb just observed as they made their way toward the middle of the bridge, lifted him up and over the railing, and let go.

He began to fall, watching the ground beneath approach with the previous victim's body underneath him. And just in the moment he was about to hit the ground, he squinted his eyes, and let out a sharp scream.

"Ahhhhhhh. Aaahhhhh. Aaaaahhhhh. Aaaahhhhhhh."

"Someone calm him down."

"Caleb it's alright mate."

"What's he taken?"

"Aaahhhhh. Aaaahhhhhhh. Ahhh. Ah."

"Ah that's right, Ah. Breathe out, it's alright mate," Gibson said.

"What happened," Caleb asked.

"We just got here, what'd you take?"

Caleb rubbed his eyes in confusion. "I just had some salvia," he said, "I didn't think it was enough to take me out though."

“You all good?”

“Fuck hey, what the fuck!” Caleb said as he rubbed his head, trying to understand what had happened, what was real, and when and where he was.

“Intense hey?” Gibson said as he looked over at Steve.

“We’ll give you a moment, but we were just wanting to get some acid, if you have any?”

“Sure sure… acid yep…” Caleb got up, and began opening drawers of his cupboard, looking through bottles of powders and liquid to find it, “what’s the occasion?” he asked, anticipating the story of the bridge, the performances, and the whole chain of events that followed.

“We uhh,” Steve began speaking, “can’t tell you.”

“Reminds me of a nap sandwich,” Caleb said.

www.ingramcontent.com/pod-product-compliance
Lightning Source LLC
LaVergne TN
LVHW050940080826
845145LV00004B/1347